Look at the Baby

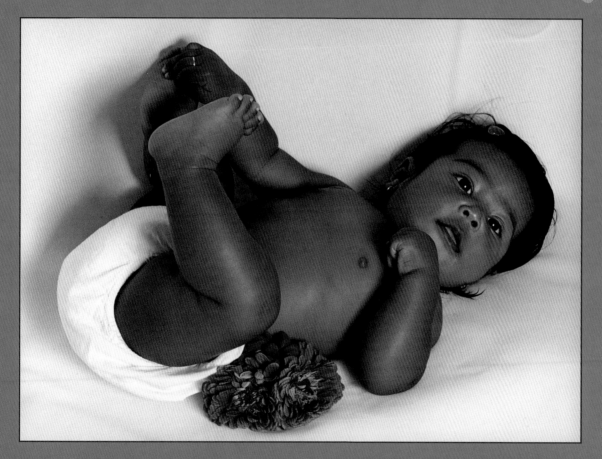

Kelly Johnson

Henry Holt and Company / New York

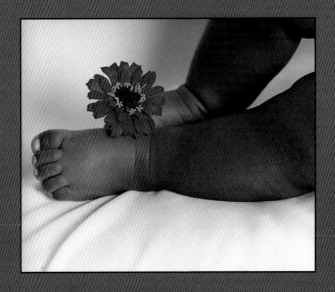

Henry Holt and Company, LLC
Publishers since 1866
115 West 18th Street
New York, New York 10011
www.henryholt.com

Henry Holt is a registered trademark of Henry Holt and Company, LLC

Library of Congress Cataloging-in-Publication Data
Johnson, Kelly.
Look at the baby / Kelly Johnson.
Summary: Pictures and a simple rhyme celebrate babies,
from their tiny toes to their round cheeks.
[1. Babies—Fiction. 2. Stories in rhyme.] I. Title.
PZ8.3.J63353 Lo 2002   [E]—dc21   2001005204
ISBN 0-8050-6522-9 / First Edition—2002
Designed by Martha Rago
Printed in the United States of America on acid-free paper. ∞
1 3 5 7 9 10 8 6 4 2

My deepest thanks
to my husband, Thiel (Bruce) Johnson,
for his endless support, understanding, and love.
To my beautiful daughters, Natasha and Nicole—thank you so much
for your sharing, warmth, and love. To my family—J. T. and Gloria Tims,
Kimberly Brown, Adrian and Aaron Stelly, Byron Brown Jr., Rose Bryant,
Shirley R. Orr, Lester and Thelma Johnson—thank you for sharing
your immeasurable wisdom, generosity, and love. Love you all.
To the parents and babies—Byron, Shalonda, and Brandon Brown;
Ryan, Jennifer, and Jalen Williams; Sioni, Lolinita,
and Silina Malua; Rob, Lisa, and Mya India Thomas;
Micaiah Alexander, Kenneth Staples, and Phyllis Whitmore—
thank you for trusting me to photograph your beautiful children.
May God bless you all.
And many thanks to Laura Godwin, Martha Rago,
and Reka Simonsen at Henry Holt.

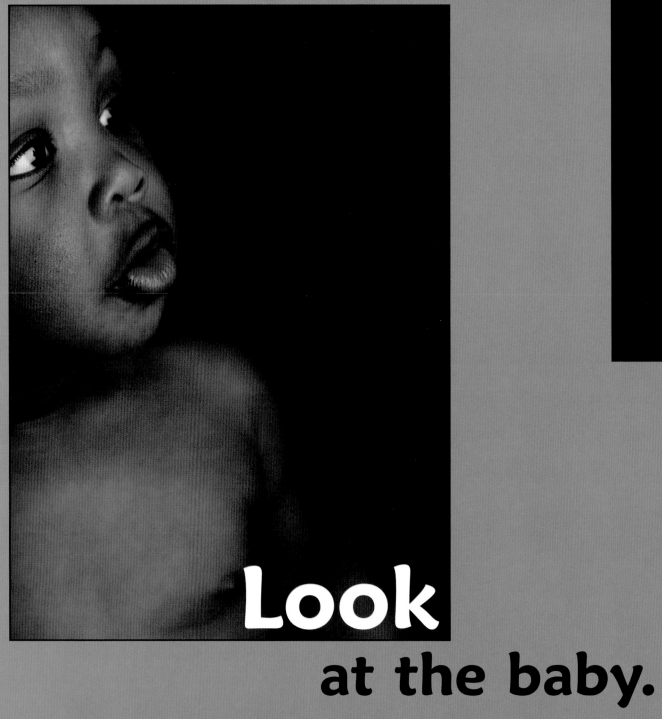

Look at the baby.

Look
at the baby's **nose.**

Look
at the baby's

fingers.

Look
at the baby's

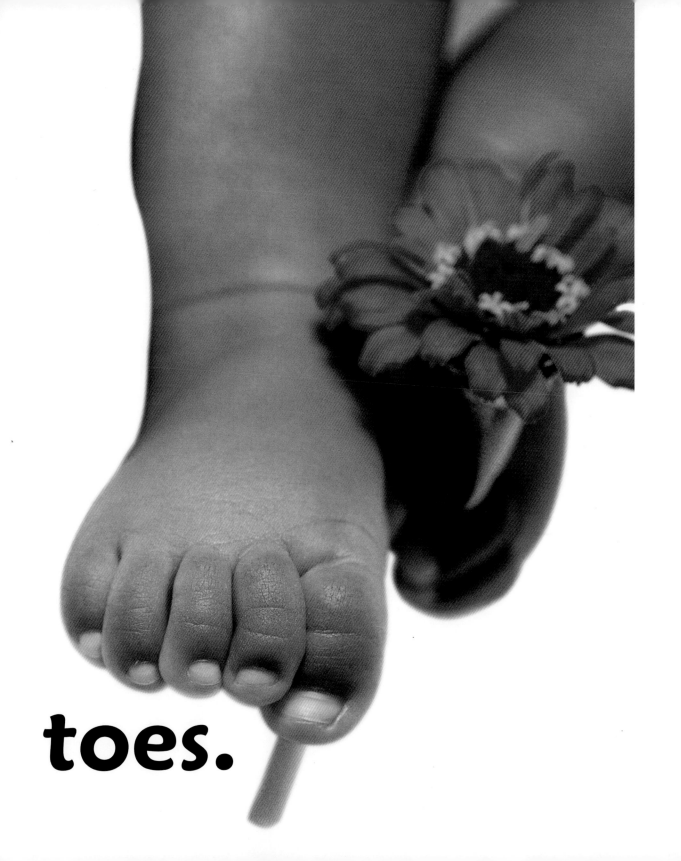

toes.

Look
at the baby's

chin.

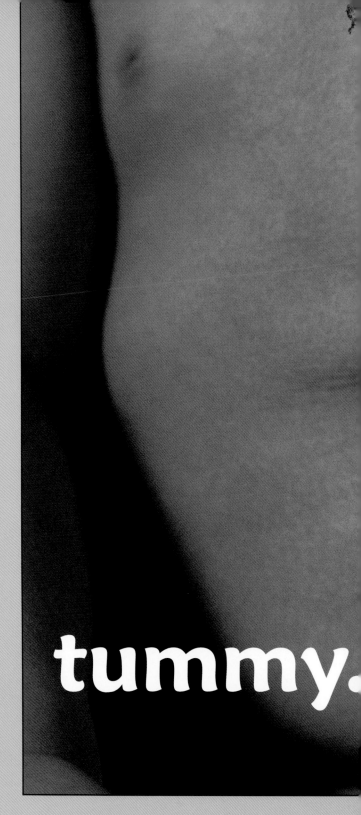

Look
at the
baby's tummy.

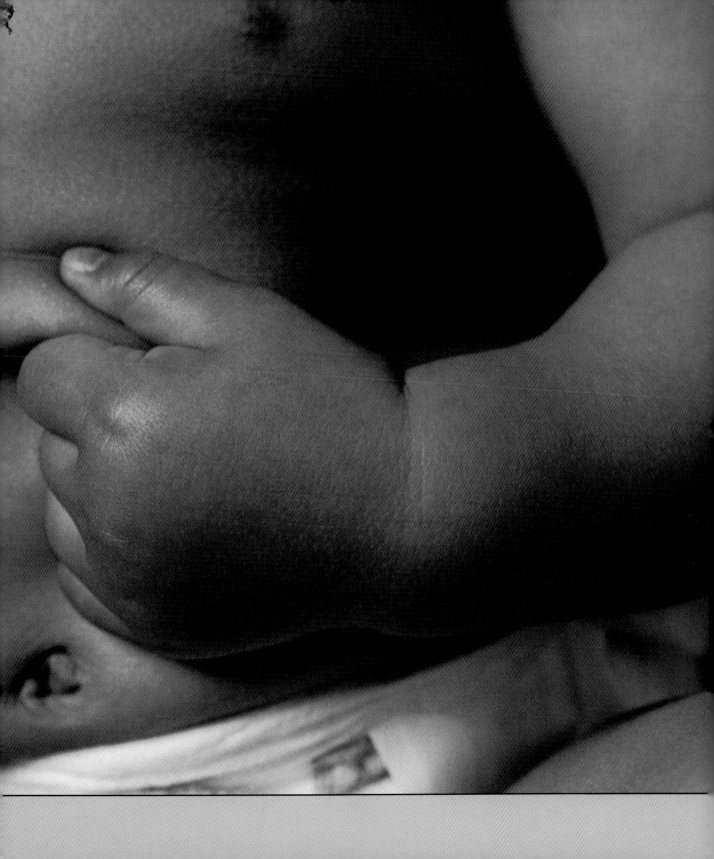

Look
at the baby's

legs.

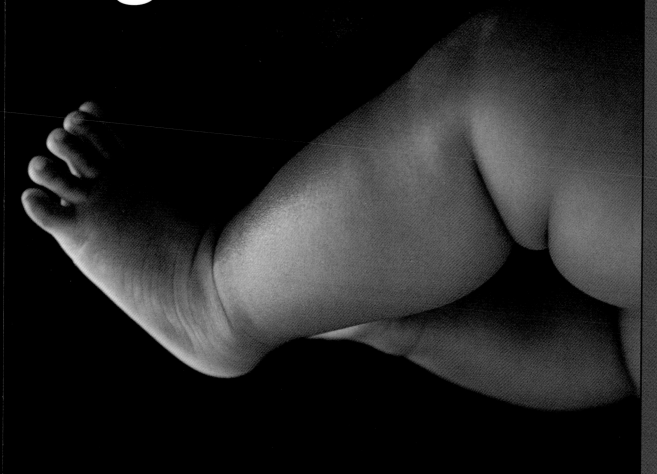

Yum, yum, yummy!

Look
at the baby's

eyes.

Look
at the baby's

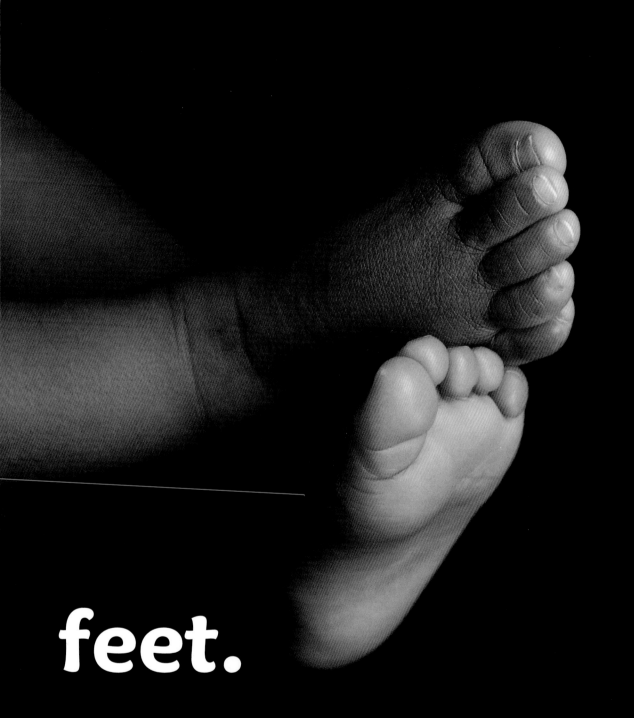

feet.

Look at the baby...

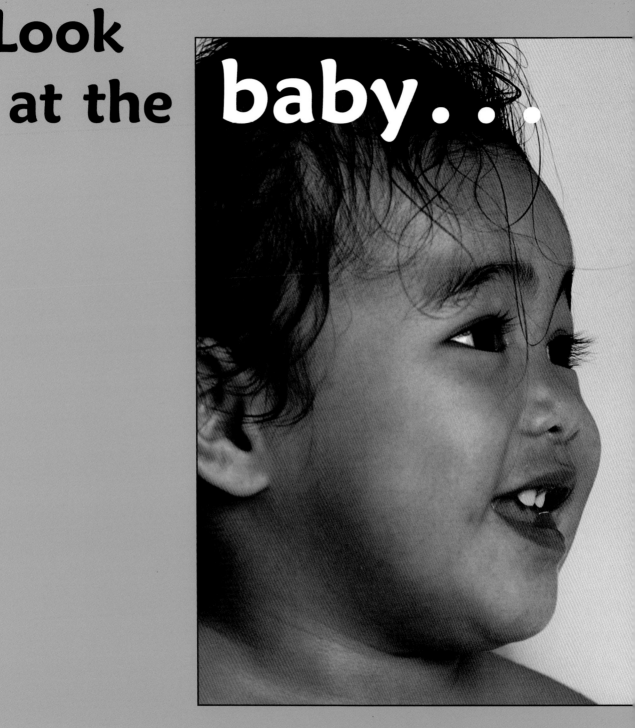

sweet, sweet, sweet!

For Olyvia
   From Grandma